The Bible Is... For Me!

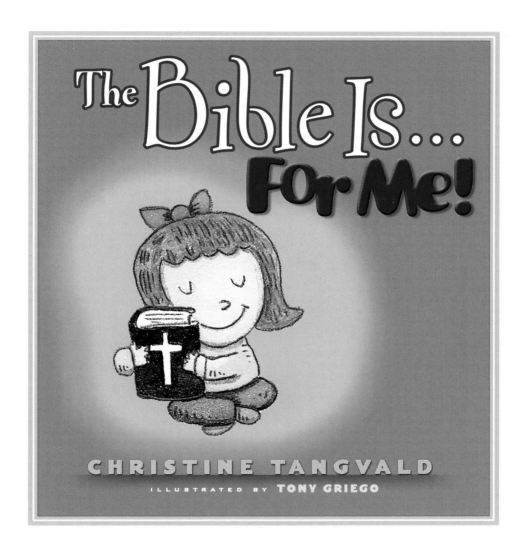

CHRISTINE TANGVALD

ILLUSTRATED BY TONY GRIEGO

BETHANY BACKYARD®
www.bethanyhouse.com

The Bible Is... For Me!

Text © 2000 by Christine Tangvald

Illustrations © 2000 by Bethany House Publishers

Design and production by Lookout Design Group, Inc. (www.lookoutdesign.com)

Published by Bethany House Publishers

A Ministry of Bethany Fellowship International

11400 Hampshire Avenue South

Minneapolis, Minnesota 55438

www.bethanyhouse.com

Printed in China.

Library of Congress Cataloging-in-Publication Number applied for

Did you know that the [Bible] is for me? IT IS!

God talks to me through the [Bible] and tells me lots of things

He wants me to know.

What is your favorite story in God's [Bible] ?

Is it the Christmas story about [baby Jesus] ?

Is it the story about [Noah's] huge [ark] ?

I LOVE to hear exciting stories from God's [Bible] , don't you?

He wrote it all . . . **For Me!**

The very first book of the Bible tells me that in the beginning,

God created the whole wide world . He DID.

God created the sun , which shines and shimmers. (It is hot!)

God created the stars, which twinkle and gleam. (They are pretty!)

God created the moon, which glimmers and glows.

(I like the moon! Don't you?)

Next, God created lots of land, green grass , tall trees ,

and huge blue oceans . Wow! God was busy, wasn't He?

God created the heavens and the earth. He did!

MATTHEW 3:17

Then God created lots of animals (*grrrr, roar, meow*) and  (*cheep, cheep, tweet*) and (*splish, splash*)

birds   fish

to live in His wonderful .

world

But God saved the best for last. Last of all, God created a and a ! He created them a lot like HIMSELF—

man   woman

in His own image! Imagine THAT!

I'm so glad God created the whole wide . . .

world

The Bible says God created
the whole wide world— **For Me!**

GENESIS 1:20-31

My tells me lots of exciting stories about God's people!

Bible

I can pretend to be on his ![ark], counting animals.

Noah   ark

1, 2 ![elephants] (*stomp, stomp!*)

elephants

1, 2 ![lions] (*roar, roar!*)

lions

1, 2 ![snakes] (*eeek, eeek!*)

snakes

1, 2 ![giraffes] (*stretch, stretch!*)

giraffes

1, 2 ![skunks] (*pew, pew!*)

skunks

1, 2 ![robins] (*cheep, cheep!*)

robins

1, 2 ![alligators] (*chomp, chomp!*)

alligators

 obeyed God. Guess what? I can obey God, too!

Noah

The Bible tells me lots of exciting stories.

GENESIS 6:14, 19, 20

I can pretend to be Moses when he stretched

out his arms over the Red Sea .

"Open wide!" commanded Moses .

The water gurgled and gushed and rushed back.

Then Moses led God's people to safety right through

the middle of the  Red Sea . It's TRUE!

WOW! I wish I could have seen that!

 Moses had faith in God. Guess what?

I can have faith in God, too!

The Bible tells me about God's people.

EXODUS 14:21-22

I can pretend to be  friend , pulling in

heavy   on his fishing  .

nets   boat

"Ooof, ugh!" Pull and tug.

"Ooof, ugh!" Pull and tug.

"Whew!" That's hard work!

" , come be my helper!" said .

Peter   Jesus

"Okay," said . "I will be your helper."

Peter

Guess what? I can be helper, too!

Jesus'

Jesus called Peter to be His helper.

MATTHEW 4:18–20

The most important person in the is .
Bible Jesus

Did you know that is God's OWN SON? He is.
Jesus

The says so!
Bible

Long, long ago, was born in a little
baby Jesus stable

in Bethlehem.

 and were there.  and
Mary Joseph Angels shepherds

and were there.
wise men

I wish I could have been there, too. Don't you?

The Bible tells me how Jesus was born.

LUKE 2:1-20; MATTHEW 2:1-2

And the 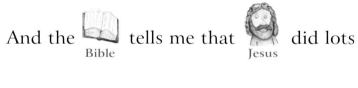 tells me that did lots

of important things.

 performed many miracles that surprised people.

Oh, yes. One time after touched the eyes

of a blind man, the man could see perfectly!

"That's amazing!" said the man. "Thank you, ."

But the most important thing the tells me is that

 is my very own FRIEND and SAVIOR! Yes, He is!

I'm GLAD is my friend and Savior, aren't you?

The Bible tells me
that Jesus is my very own friend and Savior.

LUKE 6:12–16; MARK 8:22–26; EPHESIANS 2:8,9

Did you know that the 📖 (Bible) is God's own Word . . . **For Me**? It is.

The 📖 (Bible) tells me to ❤️ (love) other people. I do.

The 📖 (Bible) tells me to be honest. I am.

The 📖 (Bible) tells me not to act mean or disobey my parents. I don't.

And the 📖 (Bible) tells me that I can talk to God about ANYTHING

I want to, ANYTIME I want to . . . ALL BY MYSELF!

The 📖 (Bible) tells me to 🙌 (PRAY). I can, and I do.

I (PRAY) !

The Bible tells me to pray.

2 TIMOTHY 3:16-17

Did you know God's Bible gives me wonderful PROMISES? It does.

God promises He loves me. He does.

God promises that He FORGIVES me. He does.

God promises that His Holy Spirit will always be with me. He is!

Isn't that great? I like these promises, don't you?

And the Bible promises that someday I will go to heaven if

I believe in God's Son, Jesus. I DO believe in Jesus! I really, really do!

Thank you, God, for the wonderful promises you have written

in your Bible ... For Me!

God's Bible gives me promises!

EPHESIANS 1:7, 3:18; JOHN 14:16; ROMANS 10:9

I'm so glad all of God's Bible is . . . For Me!

I think God's Bible is the most exciting book ever written!

Don't you?

Thank you, God, for making your Bible . . .

All of God's Bible is **For Me!**

A Bible Treasure Hunt... FOR Me!

1. Do you know HOW MANY books are in your Bible?

There are _____ books in the OLD TESTAMENT.

There are _____ books in the NEW TESTAMENT.

2. Do you know WHERE these Bible treasures are? How FAST can you find them in your Bible?

? Where is the Lord's Prayer?

? Where are the Ten Commandments?

? Where is Jesus' Sermon on the Mount?

? Where are the Beatitudes?

? Can you find the Christmas story?

? How fast can you find the 23rd Psalm?

GOOD FOR YOU!

3. What book in your Bible is a book of songs of PRAISE?

4. What book in your Bible is full of WISDOM?

5. Can you find a whole chapter in your Bible on LOVE?

3. Psalms 4. Proverbs 5. 1 Corinthians 13

Psalm 23
Christmas story - Luke 2
Beatitudes - Matthew 5 : 3–11
Sermon on the Mount - Matthew 5–7
Ten Commandments - Exodus 20
2. Lord's Prayer - Matthew 6 : 9–13

1. 66 total (39 Old Testament; 27 New Testament)

I'm so glad God's Bible is... FOR Me!